SOPHIE AND THE NEW BABY

Catherine and Laurence Anholt

ORCHARD BOOKS

For Joan, with much love.

Visit Catherine and Laurence Anholt's website at
www.anholt.co.uk

ORCHARD BOOKS
338 Euston Road, London NWI 3BH
Orchard Books Australia
Level 17-207 Kent Street, Sydney, NSW 2000

First published in 1995 by Orchard Books
This edition published in 2010

ISBN 978 1 40830 213 2

A CIP catalogue record for this book
is available from the British Library.

1 3 5 7 9 10 8 6 4 2
Printed in China

Orchard Books is a division of Hachette Children's Books,
an Hachette UK company.
www.hachette.co.uk

The very first flower pushed its way through the melting snow.
Sophie ran to look, then carefully lifted her rag doll from the pram.
"Look," she told her, "spring is here."

Sophie and her mum and dad walked further into the woods. After a while, Sophie's mum told her a secret. A BIG, IMPORTANT secret.

"Guess what, Sophie?" she said. "Soon you'll have a real little person to play with. We're going to have another baby. What do you think of that?"

"Will it be at home when we get back?" asked Sophie.
Her dad laughed. "No," he said. "We'll have to wait until
the winter. It will be a Winter Baby."

Right through the summer, Sophie waited for the new baby. In the hot evenings, she took her doll to bed and gave her the best place on her pillow. "You'll have to move over," she told the other toys. "Someone important is coming soon."

Sophie had never waited so long for anything. Sometimes she forgot all about the Winter Baby.

One day, a big brown leaf floated down from the golden trees. Sophie ran to catch it. The leaf drifted slowly from side to side, then it landed gently in the pram, right next to Sophie's doll.

Her dad smiled. "Now it's autumn," he said. "The baby will be here soon."

Sophie helped her mum get the baby's room ready. Her dad brought down a little crib that used to be Sophie's, but Sophie was far too big for it now. Next to the crib, she made a bed for her own rag doll.

The afternoons were dark. Sophie and her dad played indoors.
Outside the bare branches were white with frost. Sophie dressed her
doll in warm clothes and carried her carefully, just like a real baby.

Very late one night, Sophie sat up in bed.
Something was different.
Something was coming.

"Why is everything so quiet?"
Sophie asked her doll.
She tiptoed downstairs.

Her dad was looking out of the window.

He put his arm around her.

"Look, Sophie," he whispered. "It's going to snow."

Sophie looked out at the moonlight. She saw the very first snowflake floating slowly out of the silent sky.

Sophie wished she could stay like that forever.
Just her and her dad, watching the world turn white.

That night, her brother was born.

At first, the baby slept all day. His face was wrinkled as if he'd been in the bath too long. Sometimes he yawned a huge yawn, then Sophie leant over and kissed him. She smelt his special new baby smell and stroked his soft warm face.

But on other days, her brother cried. He waved his little hands
in the air and yelled. Sophie brought him all her toys, she even
showed him the rag doll, but her brother wasn't interested.

He wanted to be fed, he wanted to be changed, he wanted
to be cuddled and he wanted it *right now*.

"When will he be going back again?" Sophie asked her mum.
Sophie's mum laughed. "This baby isn't going back," she said.
"He's here forever. We can't just put him away like your rag doll."

Sophie wanted someone to help her build a snowman,
or go for a walk with her in the woods, but her mum
and her dad were too busy with the baby.

Sophie pointed at her brother. "You said he could
play with me," she said.

"You'll have to wait a while, Sophie," said her dad.
"He's not big enough yet."
"I ALWAYS have to wait," shouted Sophie.
So she took her doll and went out by herself,
slamming the door behind.

The garden was quiet and empty. Sophie bent down and began
to play sadly by herself. She built a little snowman.

The sky turned grey and the snow fell faster and faster around her.

"You're all alone and cold," she told the snowman, "just like me."

Sophie began to cry. Her tears splashed onto the snow. She looked
up at the house where the windows were bright.

Inside her mum and dad were smiling down at the new baby.

Sophie threw down her rag doll and shouted at the sky . . .

She cried so much, she didn't see her dad coming across the garden. He lifted her up in his big arms and held her close.

"I know it's difficult, Sophie," he said. "Everything's changed for you."

In the kitchen, Sophie's mum made her a warm drink.
"Did you lose your doll?" she asked.
"Yes," sniffed Sophie. "And I don't care."
The rag doll lay forgotten in the snow.

A long time passed before Sophie got used to the Winter
Baby. He began to make little happy noises when he saw
Sophie and held tightly onto her finger, and then, at last,
it was Sophie who taught him to smile.

Very early one morning,
Sophie sat up in bed.
Something was different.
Something was coming.

Sophie tiptoed downstairs.

Her dad was looking out of the window.

He put his arm around her. "Look, Sophie,"
he whispered. "It's springtime again!"
Sophie looked outside. The snow had melted.
She felt a warm feeling inside.

Right in the middle of the garden, exactly where the snowman had been, Sophie thought she could see a flower: the first flower of spring.

She ran outside to pick it for her little brother. He had never seen spring before.

But when she got close, Sophie found it wasn't a flower after all. It was a doll. Her own rag doll.

Sophie washed and dried the doll and dressed her in new clothes.

When they went walking, Sophie gave the rag doll to her brother.
"I don't need this any more," she told him. "I've got you to play
with now."

All through the woods, the new leaves were opening and the sun
shone through the trees. It was the start of a whole new year – for
Sophie and the Winter Baby.